This book belongs to:

....

....

Quarto is the authority on a wide range of topics.

Quarto educates, entertains and enriches the lives of
our readers—enthusiasts and lovers of hands-on living.

www.quartoknows.com

Editor: Carly Madden
Designer: Hannah Mason
Series Designer: Victoria Kimonidou
Editorial Director: Victoria Garrard
Art Director: Laura Roberts-Jensen

First published in hardback in the UK in 2015
by QED Publishing
Part of The Quarto Group
The Old Brewery, 6 Blundell Street, London N7 9BH

A catalogue record for this book is available from the British Library.

ISBN 978 1 78493 129 2

Printed in China

Rapunzel, Rapunzel, WASH YOUR HAIR!

Written by Steve Smallman

Illustrated by Neil Price

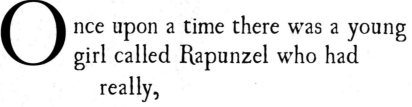

Once upon a time there was a young
girl called Rapunzel who had
really,

really

long

hair!

She'd been kidnapped by
a wicked witch who kept
her in a room at the top
of a very tall tower.

The tower had no staircase
and no front door!

The wicked witch used
Rapunzel's hair as a rope to
climb up and down the tower.

When she needed to
climb up she cried,
"Rapunzel, Rapunzel,
let down your
golden hair!"

The hair fell down and
the witch climbed up.
OUCH!

Poor Rapunzel never went out at all.
She was sad, lonely...

...and very hairy!

Having so much hair
was hard work.

Rapunzel was
always tripping
over her hair.

It was such an effort to wash
and brush that, after a while,
she just didn't bother!

She sat by the
window daydreaming
about being rescued
by a handsome prince.
Her hair got dirtier
and dirtier.

One day, a handsome prince called Boris heard Rapunzel singing. He followed the sound to the tower.

He tried to climb the tower but it was too smooth and he couldn't get a grip!

Then he heard the wicked witch coming
and hid behind a bush. She called out,

"Rapunzel, Rapunzel,
let down your
golden hair!"

The hair came
down and the witch
climbed up. OUCH!

Boris waited for the witch to climb back down.
Then, when he was sure she was gone,
he sneaked up to the tower and in his best
'wicked witch' voice cried,

"Rapunzel, Rapunzel,
let down your
golden hair!"

The hair came down
but it was filthy.

"Yuck!" he cried.
"I'm not climbing
up that!"

He stomped off
in a huff!

A few days later, another prince came along.

Albert had heard about the girl in
the tower with the lovely voice
and the disgusting hair.

So he came to rescue her...
with gloves on. He called out,
"Rapunzel, Rapunzel,
let down your
golden hair!"

The hair came down and he started climbing up...

...but halfway up the tower, his head started to itch! He'd caught head lice from Rapunzel's hair!

He let go of her hair to scratch his head and fell back down with a thump! He gave up and left.

Rapunzel's hair got so grubby
and grim that even the
witch couldn't stand
it anymore.

"I'm leaving!"
screeched the witch.
"And I won't
be coming back!"

She climbed down Rapunzel's
hair for the last time.

It was so greasy
that she lost her grip
and slipped to the bottom
of the tower with a
SPLAT!

Soon another prince came along. His name was
Alistair and he had a ladder. He called out,

"Rapunzel, Rapunzel,
let down your golden hair!"

The hair came down and
Alistair gasped in horror!

"Oh my goodness!"
he cried.

"Your hair needs rescuing more than you do! When did you last use shampoo?"

He fetched a hosepipe, head-lice lotion, shampoo, conditioner...

...and a selection of brushes and combs.

Alistair set to work!

It took all day, but by the time Alistair had finished, Rapunzel's hair was clean, shiny, golden and beautiful.

Then the prince helped Rapunzel climb out of the tower.

"Oh, thank you, my handsome prince!" sighed Rapunzel.

"You have saved
me, and my hair.
I suppose you'll want
to marry me now?"

"No, thanks,"
said the prince,
"but would you
like a haircut?"

Rapunzel had her
hair cut short.

It looked terrific
and was so much
easier to wash.

In fact, she kept it so clean
and healthy that the prince gave
her a job in his hair salon!

Prince Alistair used Rapunzel's leftover hair to make wigs and moustaches for all the bald people of the kingdom...

...who all lived happily and hairily ever after!

Next steps

Show the children the cover again. When they first saw it, did they think that they already knew the story? How is this story different from the traditional story? Which bits are the same?

Rapunzel's hair was really long. Ask the children to imagine what it would be like to have hair that length. Would it be easy to look after? How long would it take to wash and brush? What if it got tangles in it?

In this story, did Rapunzel look after her hair? Ask the children what they think it would feel like to have really dirty hair.

What happened when the first prince saw Rapunzel's hair? What did he say?

What happened when the second prince tried to climb up Rapunzel's hair?

When the third prince came along, what did the children think he would do when he saw Rapunzel's yucky hair? What did he actually do?

When Prince Alistair had washed and brushed Rapunzel's hair, how did it look? How did Rapunzel feel?

Ask the children to draw a picture of themselves with really long hair like Rapunzel. Or they could draw themselves with a really big moustache – like the ones that Alistair made with Rapunzel's leftover hair!